10
Minute Tales

THOMAS
& FRIENDS™

Based on *The Railway Series* by the Rev. W. Awdry

When you see these symbols:

Read aloud
Read aloud to
your child.

Read alone
Support your child
as they read alone.

Read along
Read along with
your child.

EGMONT
We bring stories to life

One day, Thomas was waiting for his passengers at Maithwaite Station. Percy puffed up with The Fat Controller on board.

"Thomas, I need you to collect a very important passenger," said The Fat Controller. "He's a Fireman who rescued Lady Hatt's cat from a tree."

"He's a hero!" tooted Percy.

"We're going to give him a medal here today for helping others," added The Fat Controller.

"Yes, Sir!" Thomas peeped.

Thomas had a new job to do.
He had to bring the hero to the station.

Read alone

Thomas pulled away from the station and chuffed through the countryside to collect the Fireman.

"It must be very exciting to be a hero," Thomas puffed to himself. "I'm going to try to be a Really Useful Engine. If an engine's in trouble, I'll be ready to help!"

"Ready to help! Ready to help!" sang Annie and Clarabel.

Thomas wanted to be a hero too.
He was ready to help.

Along the way, Thomas saw lots of children waiting at the bus stop.

"We're going to see the hero," said Alice from High Farm. "Bertie the Bus is taking us to the medal ceremony."

"I'm on my way to pick him up now!" Thomas replied, proudly.

Read alone

Thomas saw some children at the bus stop.
They were going to see the hero too.

As Thomas chuffed along, he saw that a tree had fallen across the tracks next to him. This was very dangerous.

He backed up to the junction and told the Signalman, "There's a tree on the line. The engines must take another track!"

A tree had fallen on to the track.
Thomas asked the Signalman to help.

The Signalman quickly changed the points so that the engines would run along a different line.

Just then, Harvey raced through the junction. He looked very surprised as he changed tracks and steamed down a new line!

Thomas was pleased. "I saved Harvey!" he puffed. "Now I'm a hero too."

The Signalman changed the points.
Harvey went down a new line.

Read alone

Read aloud

Read along

Thomas chuffed on to collect the Fireman. He saw Donald and Douglas stuck behind the fallen tree.

"Have you seen Harvey?" Donald asked. "We can't go anywhere until he moves this tree."

Thomas saw that he had made a mistake. "I sent him down the other track so that he wouldn't crash into the tree."

Donald and Douglas were stuck.
They needed Harvey to move the tree.

Read aloud   Read along

Donald and Douglas were cross.

"Bring back Harvey so we can finish our jobs," said Donald.

"We need Harvey!" said Douglas.

"I'm sorry," Thomas called back as he huffed down the track. "I don't have time to find Harvey. I need to collect the Fireman. He's a hero!"

Read alone

Thomas had made a mistake.
Donald and Douglas were cross.

Further down the line, Thomas saw Toby on the next track. He had broken down and couldn't move. In the distance, Thomas heard Gordon's whistle.

"Toby has broken down on the Express line, and Gordon is coming!" Thomas whistled with worry. "I must rescue Toby!"

Read alone

Toby had broken down on Gordon's track.
Thomas had to help him!

Read aloud   Read along

Thomas quickly backed up to the points and changed on to the Express line. He buffered up behind Toby and shunted him as fast as he could.

"Help!" cried Toby.

"Don't worry, Toby," puffed Thomas. "You'll be all right."

He shunted Toby into a hidden siding as Gordon steamed past.

Read alone

Thomas pushed Toby into a siding.
Gordon did not see them.

Read aloud **Read along**

"I'm a hero for rescuing you," Thomas proudly told Toby, as Gordon huffed out of view.

"No, you're not," Toby replied, crossly. "Gordon was bringing an Engineer to fix me."

Thomas had made another mistake! "I'm not a hero," he said, sadly. "And now I'm late to collect the Fireman. He'll miss his own medal ceremony."

Thomas felt terrible.

Gordon was carrying a man to fix Toby!
Now Toby was cross with Thomas, too.

Just then, Percy puffed up.

"Percy, will you go and pick up the Fireman for me?" Thomas asked. "You'll have to hurry. The medal ceremony starts very soon."

Pleased, Percy agreed and chuffed off to collect the Fireman.

Now Thomas could fix his mistakes.

Read alone

Thomas wanted to fix his mistakes.
He asked Percy to pick up the hero.

Read aloud   Read along

First, Thomas steamed after Gordon and caught up with him. Gordon was surprised when Thomas asked him to stop!

Thomas collected the Engineer and brought him back to fix Toby.

"Thank you, Thomas!" tooted Toby, as the man worked on his wheel.

"You're welcome," replied Thomas.

Thomas found Gordon.
He took the man to fix Toby.

Read aloud   **Read along**

Next, Thomas chuffed back to the line that Harvey had gone down. He found Harvey and took him to move the fallen tree.

"Thank you, Thomas!" whistled Donald and Douglas, as Harvey cleared the line. They sped down the track to finish their work.

"You're welcome," Thomas called after them. He had fixed all of his mistakes, but he knew that didn't make him a hero.

Thomas took Harvey to move the tree.
Donald and Douglas could finish their work.

Read aloud **Read along**

Thomas puffed sadly back to the engine sheds. Along the way, he saw that Bertie the Bus had stopped on the road. The children were waiting around him.

"What's the matter?" asked Thomas.

"I'm stuck in the mud," beeped Bertie, worriedly. "Will you take the children to the medal ceremony?"

"Oh yes!" peeped Thomas.

Bertie the Bus was stuck in the mud.
He could not take the children to see the hero.

Read aloud   Read along

The children climbed on board Annie and Clarabel. Thomas steamed quickly so they wouldn't miss the ceremony. They arrived at Maithwaite Station just in time!

The Fat Controller gave the medal to the Fireman.

"You are a hero," Lady Hatt told the Fireman.

"And you are our hero, Thomas!" called the children.

Thomas beamed from buffer to buffer. He was a Really Useful Engine, after all!

Read alone

Thomas took the children to see the hero.
They said Thomas was a hero too!

Enjoy more from the
10-Minute Tales range

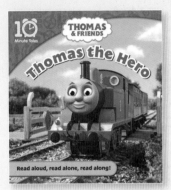

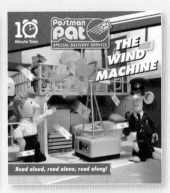

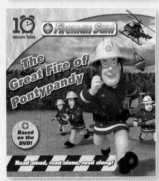

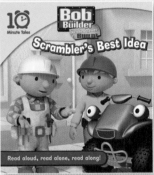

Go online at egmont.co.uk/10minutetales
for puzzles, colouring and
activities

...Ben 10 & Gormiti
10-Minute Adventures also available